Cathas

and

The Squirrel Incident

The Village

THE RECTORY
Rev & Mrs Idris Jones

PARKING FOR SHOP USERS ONLY

PROVISIONS

Ferra Peace

Eric Peace

School

Wallop
School

The
Crown Public
House

THE CROWN

Pound

Much Wallop

To the river →
And the green common

→ Spanish Gr

Walters

Church
CAR PARK

TO THE RIVER

← To Spanish Green

Margaret
ning
fea

Mr & Mrs)
Peace
+
George, Lizzy
Phoebe + Catha

Mr & Mrs
Storey

Steve and
Lucy Owens
+
Kerry (pug)

New builds

ane

Cathas

and

The Squirrel Incident

Written and Illustrated

by

Tessa Bremner

Acknowledgements

Thank you to Amanda Berry for her wonderful patterns for the dogs. Also, thanks to Kath Dalmeny @ www.ravelry.com for the pattern for the cat. I must acknowledge Deramores wool without whom, of course, the family couldn't have been knitted and last but not least Hobbycraft at Farnborough, who also sell wool plus many assorted items which have enabled me to create my little family.

Thank you also to my supportive family for showing their interest in my stories.

The greatest thanks of all must go to Eloise De Sousa for her continued support and encouragement when I almost gave up. She has edited my stories and mentored me throughout my writing.

❧Cathas❧

Mr and Mrs Peace loved living in their tucked away village of Much Wallop. Their children had grown up and now had children of their own. Mr Peace had retired from his job as a bank manager. This meant he could spend more time in the garden and, of course, with his wife. He also had time to read his books on trains.

Mrs Peace was glad he was around, well, most of the time. Her husband had his uses. Spider catching was one of them. Their main love, apart from family, was their dogs. They walked them every day on the local common and through the woods.

Although Fenna Peace loved the dogs, she had always wanted a cat. As a child, she was not allowed to have one because her mother was allergic to cat fur. Mr Peace had never shown an interest in having a feline member in the family. In fact, he didn't like them. He kept the reason for this to himself (that will be disclosed later in the story). The more Mrs Peace thought about having a cat, the more she wanted one.

It was by chance that she met her neighbour one morning whilst walking the dogs. Margaret and Trevor Winning lived at number 17 Pound Lane. Margaret had been cutting the small hedge in her front garden. The ladies started chatting about this and that was when Mrs Peace mentioned that she wanted a cat. Margaret told Fenna about their new addition to their family.

She then went on to tell her nosey neighbour about something that had happened which shocked Mrs Peace.

'Oh, if only I could persuade Eric. He doesn't like cats, apparently. Can't think why. I shall just have to deal with things myself!' said Mrs Peace.

The next day, while they were having their morning coffee, Fenna Peace repeated to her husband what Margaret had told her. She told him that Margaret and Trevor had adopted the most beautiful kitten she had ever seen. It was a tabby cat. The Winnings had decided to call him Maffeo as he was found behind an Italian restaurant.

'By the way, dear, did I mention to you why Margaret Winning had the idea of getting a cat?' Fenna did not wait for her husband to answer. 'Well, apparently, she was hanging out her washing when she saw a movement out of the corner of her eye. It was a rat! It sat there, bold as brass, chewing on bread left out for the birds. Margaret said it didn't seem to be bothered by her presence, even though she showed it the garden broom. She said it had beady eyes that just stared at her. It finally scuttled over to the shed.'

Mr Peace was going to ask his wife if Margaret had expected the rat to sweep the path. Perhaps that was why she had shown it the broom! He thought better of it – Fenna would not have found it funny. Instead, he replied, 'Really, dear? How odd!'

'Margaret and Trevor have found a lovely little kitten. I think I told you. Well, I have found a chap who has two kittens for sale. We are going to look at them this afternoon.'

Eric Peace almost dropped his book. 'What on earth for?' His reply sounded more like a scream.

'It's not that far; he lives in Spanish Green. We could get lunch out at a nice little pub somewhere.' Mrs Peace's excitement grew at the thought of getting a kitten.

Mr Butler   A Very happy Mrs Peace   An Unhappy Mr Peace.

Spanish Green

Her husband was not happy. He didn't like the idea of getting a cat. 'It's not the distance, Fenna, it's the reason for the journey!'

'Let's be honest, darling. You would have said, no way! I can't see why you have never liked cats. Just think, if one rat is watching us, there must be others close by. They have probably set up home in the shed. A cat would scare them away.' She was convinced that the argument she put forward would persuade Eric.

Fenna Peace had her way. They set off for Spanish Green. Mr Peace grudgingly entered the address into his sat nav. On the way, the road was full of big potholes which Eric was not happy about either. He was worried it would spoil his wheels. Mrs Peace told him not to worry. 'Let's find the address, dear.'

They found the cottage where the kittens lived. Mrs Peace knocked on the door and introduced herself. They were invited inside by a man called Mr Butler. He offered the couple a cup of tea which they politely turned down. Fenna's eyes were too busy spinning in her head taking in everything in the room. She loved being nosey – nothing new there!

Mr Butler told the couple that there was only one kitten left - a ginger one. The black one that Mrs Peace had expressed an interest in over the phone had been sold that morning. He carried the remaining bundle of fur out for her to see.

Fenna Peace took one look at the kitten and fell in love. They paid Mr Butler who then wrapped the kitten in a tatty piece of blanket and put him in a cardboard box. The Peace's left for home. Mr Peace spent the trip moaning about the potholes and the fact that they hadn't had any lunch. The only pub in the village was closed and Mrs Peace refused to eat burgers in a bun!

When they reached home, Fenna carried her bundle of joy inside. She wouldn't introduce him to the dogs just yet. They could do that tomorrow. The kitten's requirements were unpacked and made ready for him: a bright red litter tray, red bowls, and a new blanket in pink! There was also special milk and kitten food. This feline would have only the best.

Finally, after all the unpacking and setting up, Mr Peace got his lunch.

Mrs Peace cuddled her new addition. She told him how much she already loved him. No one would be allowed to hurt him. If they tried to cause little kitten harm, or indeed, tried to steal him, they would find out what she was capable of!

With that thought in mind, Fenna suggested to her husband that they must take the kitten to see Ted Walters. Mr Walters was an old friend. He was also the best vet (in Mrs Peace's opinion) that had ever lived. Mr Peace asked why they needed to see Ted. She replied, 'Well dear, this little fellow needs his injections to keep him well. He also needs to be microchipped so that no one can steal him from us.'

'Oh yes, of course. But having him microchipped won't stop anyone from stealing him.' Mr Peace was thinking of the bill. Having the dogs micro chipped had cost enough, but they were worth it! Did they need to microchip a cat? He didn't think so.

Fenna stroked the kitten's little pink nose. Eric wasn't interested in the little pink nose or the gold-coloured eyes. He certainly didn't want to hold him. She wanted to know why her husband didn't want to hold their new addition. He hadn't shown any interest in him - there had been no mention of the beautiful markings on the kitten's back.

Eric explained that since he was a little boy, he was afraid of cats. His grandparents had owned a cat called Wilfred. Eric loved to stroke Wilfred's soft fur and make a fuss of him. Then, one fateful day, the beloved black cat climbed onto a high shelf and leapt from it, straight onto the young Eric's back.

It clung to him, holding on with all its might, using its sharp claws. His back was seriously injured with painful scratches and memories that took a while to heal.

Ever since that day, Eric Peace has been afraid of cats.

Mrs Peace tried to console him by telling him that their innocent little kitten would never do that. He wanted to know how she could be sure of that. She told him, 'Our boy won't be allowed to climb onto high places.' Mr Peace was not convinced.

The next day, the kitten, which now had a name, was introduced to the three dogs. Mrs Peace had chosen the name, Cathas. She had recalled the time they had spent on holiday in Cornwall. The hotel they had stayed at had a cat and, according to the staff, he was an excellent mouser and caught many rats. His name had been Cathas; it was Cornish for 'cat'. He was also ginger, just like their new addition.

The dogs were not impressed with the new addition. They discussed the situation when Mother and the Squire (as they referred to Mr and Mrs Peace) went to bed.

Lizzie was the first to mention it. 'I don't see why they want a cat.'

'I like cats. I think it'd be nice to have a cat around the place,' said Phoebe.

'Have yer listened to yourself? Do you have any idea what yer talking about?' Lizzie asked her.

Phoebe replied, 'Well, I can't see the harm in it. I thought he was sweet.'

'Can't see the harm innit? Do you realise that the love they have for us will be shared? We won't get the pats on the back. We won't get treats. The money they spend on our food will be shared, so we'll get less to eat! I can't see you liking that - especially if there's a shortage of gravy! Still think it's sweet?'

'Do you really think that will happen, Lizzie?' asked George.

'Yes, I do. Look at the fuss Mother makes of Cousin Brook when he comes for a visit. That kitten will get even more fuss. They will play wiv it too! No more ball games for us!'

'Where is he now? He isn't sleeping in here,' remarked George.

'No, he ain't. That's 'cos they took 'im into their bedroom. When did we ever sleep wiv them?' Lizzie felt a growing resentment at the intrusion of the tiny bundle.

Cathas was fast asleep in his little bed, wrapped lovingly in his pink blanket. He was placed next to Mrs Peace's side of the bed. The litter tray was next door to it, just in case.

Mr Peace was reading his book when his wife asked him if he was okay. 'I am sorry, dear,' she said. 'I didn't know you were frightened of cats. You should have told me!' She paused. 'Having said that, it doesn't mean I would have changed my mind about getting him!'

Eric Peace tried to reply in a way that wouldn't upset his wife, but he was still unhappy about the whole business. 'Oh well, what's done is done. He's here now. I just hope he makes you happy.'

They each said goodnight and switched off their lamps. Mrs Peace whispered, 'Goodnight!' to little Cathas. It would appear he was already destined to be 'her boy'.

❧The Squirrel Incident❧

It was a beautiful, sunny day. Mr and Mrs Peace were enjoying a cup of tea in their neatly kept garden. Mrs Peace suggested to her husband that they could have another flower bed. She had plans for a flower bed of her own and the flowers grown in it would be hers. They would be displayed in the church where Mrs Peace was on the flower rota: a select group that arranged flowers to make the church look pretty. Her displays were the talk of the Mothers' Union.

Mr Peace was of the opinion that there was enough to do in the garden. Besides, the dogs would trample on it and Cathas (their infamous cat) would use it as his own private toilet. The discussion continued until Mr Peace dozed off in his rather comfortable chair. The three dogs were resting peacefully after their long walk on the common. On their return, they had been fed and were now content, relaxing outside with their mistress and master. The quiet was not to last.

Fenna Peace left her comfy chair and went to the kitchen to prepare the evening meal. She had called to her husband, Eric, to come in as she had found a job for him. He rubbed his eyes and reluctantly obliged.

Lizzie, one of the dogs, was the first to see Cathas creeping across the lawn. He was on route to the back door when she lifted her head to frighten off a pesky fly and noticed him. Lizzie called to George and Phoebe to look who was coming. They raised their sleepy heads to see who it was. The curious dog sat up; she wanted a better view of whatever it was dangling from Cathas' mouth.

Cathas had managed to bag himself a squirrel. This was something Lizzie had longed to achieve. She would sit for ages under a tree waiting for one to appear, but they always saw her first and did not hang around.

Cathas thought he could get past the 'devil dog', a name he often referred to when talking about Lizzie. No such luck.

Lizzie, George and Phoebe were now sitting to attention. It wasn't until the ginger feline got closer to them that they saw precisely what it was in his mouth.

Cathas stopped dead in his tracks. Lizzie, with her East-End manner, stood in front of him. She said, 'Drop it, or I'll drop you!'

The wily cat tended to be a coward, especially when facing Lizzie. He laid the unconscious critter down at her feet. Carefully placing his two front paws on the still little body, he went on to explain in his patronizing way and with his broken English accent, 'I get this for you, Senorita! I am thinking: the tail – it would look so pretty around your neck!'

'What's wrong wiv my neck? What 'av I told you? When you catch anyfing, you come and show me first. Understood, mush?'

Cathas was wishing he had gone elsewhere with his prisoner. 'Si Senorita. That's what I was going to do,' he replied in a squeaky voice.

'Well then, me old mate, why was you going the other way?' Lizzie demanded.

'No, Senorita! I no go other way. Also, pretty lady, there is nada or nothing wrong about your neck. It is so pretty. How you like the coat for your Madre?' he asked, hoping that would please her.

'Are you saying there is sumfing wrong wiv my old ma's coat?'

'Oh no, I'm not, pretty lady. I just think you could use the fur!'

Lizzie had limited patience. She was beginning to lose it. The cat that tells anyone who would listen that he came from Spain was doing her head in! 'Look, let 'im go and we will say no more about it. What do yer say?' She had now put her front paws on the still body.

'Well, what if we share him? You have the tail, and I have the rest of him. That would be good. No?'

'Are you deaf or sumfing? Did you not hear me tell you to let 'im go?' Lizzie was really annoyed.

Cathas wouldn't give up. He persisted to suggest she needed a scarf, or a fur coat, for her mother.

'I keep telling yer, I don't need nuffing for my neck. My old Ma don't need no coat. She has one.'

The discussion was becoming too much for George. He stood up and walked towards the back door. Phoebe, on the other hand, wanted to know if there was owt to eat. Having been told, no, there wasn't, she asked what Cathas had there then.

'What does it look like?' asked her annoyed sister.

'It looks like a squirrel,' answered Phoebe.

'Yes, that's because it is! But Puss in Boots here, won't give it up. Keeps telling me I need a scarf or a coat.'

'Don't you, then?' Phoebe thought that was funny, but the look from Lizzie told her it wasn't. So, she sat and watched to see what the outcome would be.

Cathas suggested other ideas as to how the poor little creature's fur could be used. The squirrel had begun to regain consciousness. He opened his eyes and looked up at his jailer. Cathas gazed down at him. Their eyes met. Cathas jumped, lifting both paws in the air. He hadn't been expecting the eyes to open. He thought the rodent was dead.

The squirrel gave a little cough and tried to speak.

'Look! He is alive!' blurted out Cathas.

Lizzie looked down at the trembling captive. She gave him a look of: *you will soon belong to me, my beauty*! 'Well? Do yer want me to finish him off, then?' she asked Cathas.

A tiny gulp could be heard coming from the squirrel's now very dry throat. He started to speak, faintly at first, then his voice became a little stronger. 'My name is Angus,' the little fellow managed to say in between coughs.

Cathas wanted to know why Angus wasn't dead. He didn't understand it.

Lizzie replied, 'Well, I thought he was proper done for. But, 'ere he is, alive and soon to be dead!'

'You don't want to eat me, lassie. I'm not very meaty. In fact, I would be quite chewy,' Angus replied, deciding it was best to plead with his captors. 'I need to get home to ma bonnie sow. She will be making ma favourite meal: acorn surprise.' His accent was very strong.

'Hang on a minute. First of all, chief, my name isn't lassie! I am not a soppy, one-time acting Collie. I am a Jack Russell. My name is Elizabeth – friends call me Lizzie. You can call me Elizabeth! While we're at it, why do yer speak the way you do?'

'Oh, that's easy! I'm from bonnie Scotland; we all speak like this.' Angus was hoping this would buy him time. There was a chance he would be able to get loose as he'd come to realise that he was dealing with a couple of cabbage brains!

Cathas asked, 'Why do you call Bonnie a sow? Is that not a lady pig?'

'It may well be, but a female squirrel is called a sow too. Actually, her name isn't Bonnie – it's Jean. That's how we Scottish tell our wives we think they're pretty.' He added, 'A baby squirrel is called a kitten by the way, and I am a boar.'

'Que? I don't find you a bore; I find you entertaining. But tell me, Senor Angus, how you have the kittens? You are not the cat.' Cathas was very confused.

Angus noticed that he was no longer held down by fur paws, so he sat upright. Lizzie told him not to get any funny ideas. She meant, of course, not to try to escape.

Phoebe now had a question. 'Can I ask yer: why is it called acorn surprise? And do yer have gravy on it? I luv gravy, me. It runs down me beard and I lick it off for ages!'

Angus grinned. 'The surprise is, there are no acorns in it. No, there isn't any gravy either.' He was convinced these creatures were a little odd.

'Why must yer always go on about food? You never stop. It's gravy this and gravy that. If you stopped asking silly questions, we could get on and eat 'im!' Lizzie growled. She was worried something would go wrong.

'I luv food, me. In fact, I'm a conifer of food!' Phoebe added with a sigh.

'You're a wha'?' asked Lizzie, really annoyed by Phoebe's interruptions.

'I'm a conifer of food.'

'You great numpty! It's a connoisseur!' Lizzie snapped. She knew that word because Mother had mentioned it to the Squire when discussing her knowledge of cooking.

Angus took the opportunity to tell them all about his family. He thought he would bore them so much that they would give up. He finished off his story by telling them how the grey squirrels sent the red squirrels away. He also informed them that the Latin name for a squirrel was *Sciurus carolinensis*.

Lizzie wanted to know why she had never been able to catch one. Angus kindly explained that squirrels could leap from tree to tree. They could also run down a tree headfirst. This was because their ankles can rotate 180 degrees.

Cathas was now fed up with all the chatter. He started to wash his face. Angus realised that both the cat and the rough speaking

Jack Russell were distracted. His eyes started doing cartwheels in his head looking around for the quickest and safest route out. He needed to act fast if he was going to get away. After all, the smart little rodent didn't want to end up covered in gravy! Cathas, now cleaning himself, and Lizzie, trying to catch another annoying fly, gave Angus the perfect opportunity to run.

With one quick flick of his bushy tail and the feeling back in his little legs, the Scottish squirrel was gone. Over the fence and home to his drey; home to his bonnie sow and his kittens. The next time he went out searching for food, he would take more care.

Lizzie couldn't believe it. How had it happened? She knew whose fault it was: Cathas. 'Why did yer take your paws off 'im? You were too busy washing that ugly mug of yours,' she snapped.

'Then why were you trying to catch the fly? Your mouth - it is big enough – so how you miss?' Cathas retorted, preparing to run. After his next remark, he knew he would have to.

'Anyway, you know how I told you, you are pretty? I lied. You are not. In fact, Senorita, you have the face like the back end of the Chihuahua!'

With that, Cathas retreated to the shed roof where the furious Jack Russell could not reach him. Lizzie was fuming. 'What did he call me?'

'Eee, I don't know. I'm off in to see if there's owt to eat. Maybe they had gravy on their dinner.' Phoebe hoped they did.

Lizzie sat for a while reflecting on the afternoon's events. She couldn't quite understand how it had all gone so very wrong. If only she had dealt with Angus sooner. If only Cathas had been more switched on!

Oh well, there was no use in, if only's.

About the Author

Tessa has always loved animals and believed they spoke to one another in their own way. She entertained her children when they were young with various stories of the antics their dogs and cat would get up to.

Some of the stories are actually true, especially the squirrel incident. Living at the back of woodland in leafy Berkshire it made it easy to create the squirrel story when their cat brought one home! When she was telling these canine and feline adventures, never in her wildest dreams did she ever imagine they would turn into books. She met a very supportive friend, Eloise, who encouraged her to put pen to paper and to learn how to use the laptop!

The Peace family became very real to her, and she has knitted the whole family. Tessa sits them around her and taps away on the keys of her laptop which has now become an instrument of necessity.

Tessa hopes you enjoy reading the stories as much as her three grandchildren do and that you like the little family that has become a big part of hers.